The Two Moons

By Lilly Williams

Note from Author

This is a work of fiction. If any names that resemble real people or persons – either living or dead - it is purely coincidental.

Mute Moon

Mute moon
Stares down in silence

Like
A woman scarred
Stripped of her dignity
Too afraid to speak

Like
A deprived child
Hungry, grieving and waiting
Too tired to speak

Like
A King enthroned
Looking at his eager subjects
Aloof in silence

Like
An enlightened scientist
Holding secrets of the future
But bound by an oath of silence

Like
A wrinkled wise old man
Concealing secrets of the past
Better left unsaid

Wise moon
Mute moon
Stares down in silence

Chapter 1

It was over. The world had come to an end. Bringing relief to millions. As for the survivors, it was the beginning of a nightmare.

Mans' greed and selfishness had won in the end, the beautiful blue planet was destroyed. There wasn't a decent place to live anymore, all the forests were gone, the oceans were totally polluted - no sea creature survived. Every month there was a disaster of some kind happening in the world - floods, droughts, earthquakes, volcano eruptions, tornados and hurricanes, tsunamis and the list went on and on. The media would have been overwhelmed - if there were media institutions to report them.

Some countries were wiped right out of the map. The refugee crisis was beyond comprehension. The countries that were left were under unimaginable crisis. Diseases and pandemics ravaged every city, town and village, the medical communities were overwhelmed and many in that sector committed suicide due to mental stress. The pharmaceutical organizations were worse hit as the mobs set fire to their buildings and laboratories, creating a shortage of medical supplies worldwide. "Big pharma" as they were known were no longer Big, they had dwindled into tiny small businesses scattered everywhere - operating in secrecy. A single painkiller pill was nearly as expensive as gold itself. Vaccines were a mere memory of the world gone by.

War was rampant as the blame shifted from one organization to another. Wounded and traumatised people needed someone to blame, and there weren't two people who agreed on who or what was responsible. There wasn't a home where grief was lacking. It was a blessed home that had three dead. Many families were wiped out entirely. Insecurity wasn't the biggest concern for many people - although padlocks were sold out in all shops and new millionaires had briefly emerged from those who provided security solutions to those who could afford them - the new millionaires didn't last long either.

Cities had turned into slams, the rich were no more, and everyone was poor. The prophets were venerated. They had predicted the end of the world for centuries and it had come to pass. Only it wasn't a sudden quick event as they had predicted. The end took its time. Seven years to be exact. It was a very long, scary, drawn-out death of our modern life. By the time the aliens arrived, people were too sick, hungry, and tired to care or be scared. There was no resistance at all. As their silver crafts flew everywhere, no one objected. Not any government, army, or activists. None. No one knew where they had come from, no one cared. Not only were people expecting the earth to combust and go out in flames, but many were also praying for it. But no one expected what was to follow. Even the doomsday prophets couldn't have seen this one coming. It was the worse yet.

.   .   .   .

Every night she dreamed she was flying. The story was different each time, but it followed the same narrative. Something horrible had happened and everyone needed to be rescued, they would come to attack her, and in that instant, she got the skills to fly, and she flew away to safety. No matter how they chased her, they couldn't catch up. She flew up and away from danger. Light as a feather, drifting in the wind.

Ruth sat on the edge of the mountain, wondering if she really can fly. If she threw herself off the edge, would she fly or fall? She came here every week to enjoy the view but mostly to ponder about her recurring dream. The view was magnificent. There was a river down below, surrounded by a forest. She imagined herself flying over the waters almost touching the surface, then swooping up very quickly. In her mind, she flew over the trees, going faster and faster over the forest, turning and twisting and twirling. Floating over the air, free as a bird.

She sat there for hours. Ruth was unmarried and childless. Not a good thing in a world where there was no sickness. Or bareness. What was wrong with her? All the women her age had at least four children. With each passing year, she became more of a loner. She didn't belong. Her husband had left her after three years. It only took three months to carry a child from conception to birth. Three months. Three years is a long time for a husband to wait. And he had waited long enough. Now he had three children with his new wife. She should feel pained by the experience, but she didn't. What was wrong with her? Why did it feel right that she was barren? And why did it bother her that three months of pregnancy didn't sound right for a human?

Ruth looked up at the orange skyline. The sun was setting, the second moon was rising. The first moon however was always in the sky. It never rose nor set. It was always there. Strange. She was always drawn to the permanent moon above. Never really shifting its position from dusk to dawn. Why did the other heavenly bodies move as the day and night progressed, but not this one?

What was wrong with it? It stood in the sky staring down at them without blinking.

She stretched out on the soft grass, lying on her back and using her hands as a pillow. She looked up at the darkening sky. She was safe, nothing bad, wicked or violent ever happened in their land. It was so peaceful. No police, courts or prisons. No one ever broke the law. She could lay there the whole night and no evil would ever befall her. This was indeed paradise. And yet she felt hollow inside like she was living a dream and her dreams were the real life.

She took a deep breath; the air was so fresh and relaxing. Although it was getting dark, it wasn't getting cold. It was always warm, day and night. Even when it rained, it was warm. She wondered about that. The sun was way below the horizon now, leaving behind a glowing orange and purple sky. Absolutely stunning! Instead of obsessing with her dreams maybe she could learn to paint and replicate those colours, she thought.

The second moon was rising and heading straight for the motionless moon. Heading for a collision. The first moon was white and looked like a feather in a cloud. Its colour never varied from day to day. Its size either. The rising moon was the mysterious moon, it changed in size and colour from week to week. It went through a recurring circle every twenty-eight days. She loved to observe it every day. This moon was like an old mute lady dying to reveal a deep secret. Doing her best to speak without words. Was she listening?

The two moons were getting closer to each other, there is going to be an eclipse. The realization of what was about to happen made her sit up straight. Was everyone watching this? She wanted to run and tell someone; she felt the urge to experience this natural phenomenon with someone else. There was no one close. She was far from any settlement. She stared at the two moons as they began touching. It sent a strange sensation down her body. Something wasn't right. She felt strange, she was dizzy. No one ever got sick, so why was she feeling dizzy. Suddenly she was fatigued, her eyes closed involuntarily. Her head was heavy, very heavy. She had to lay down again, supporting her head with her hands. And that's when it happened.

.   .   .   .

Nabi was all alone. Everyone in her family had either died of the pandemic, drought, or the many other disasters that kept attacking her village. Some died from the starvation that followed. It took seven years to lose every single person she loved and the ones that loved her. She buried far too many of them at such a tender age. Her brother died first in the earthquake. The first death is the hardest. It hit her heart just like the earthquake. The tremors lasted for weeks in her village, in her heart they had lasted for years. There is nothing like the death of a mother, she lost her mother to the pandemic. The pain was excruciating. The virus that broke out was cruel, infecting the whole earth, and spreading quickly through each continent. And just as fast it engulfed her mother's body, killing her quickly. Thankfully. Others were not so fortunate. They lasted for months in agonizing pain, little by little withering away like a blade of grass in the summer. Shrinking away in agony. In her village they called the virus "Better-yesterday" for each day was worse than the day before.

Nabi was starving, the hunger pangs were unbearable. It was too much for a seventeen-year-old to endure. She was too young to be alone, and yet the cruelty of recent years had aged her. Pushing the pain deep within her body and her mind she bends down to pick the little plant that was miraculously growing on the pavement. How come no one saw it before? It was hard to find any plant nowadays. They were all eaten. She didn't care if it was poisonous or not. In fact, she wished it was poisonous, it would be a double blessing. Satisfy her hunger and taking her life at the same time. Nabi was so weak it was a struggle to uproot it. This little plant was putting up a hard fight. What was it fighting for? Couldn't it see there was nothing to live for? She tried again, and just then she saw it. The silver plane.

Was she hallucinating? Planes had stopped flying years ago. Her sight wasn't what it was but this particular one didn't quite look like a plane. She must be hallucinating she concluded. It had been ten days since her last meal, surviving on the rainwater that people stored in what was once garbage bins. Then another one flew by. She sat down and looked up. There were hundreds of them. Silver looking aircrafts, like nothing she had seen before. They didn't move like planes either, they moved like dragonflies, coming to a complete stop in mid-air and even going in reverse. Others seem to just melt away in thin air and vanish.

One of them was hovering above her. There was a blinding flash of blue light. She lost consciousness.

.   .   .   .

Chapter 2

The alien invasion had happened. The Kamblas were here. It wasn't so much an invasion as a walkover. There was no human resistance. The survivors had been weakened by hunger. It was just as their leader had said, patience would be their most effective weapon. The humans' greed and selfishness had ruined their planet. As the earth got sicker and sicker, so did the humans. They were killing the earth, and in its last act to save itself, the earth was killing the humans. The Kamblas watched this drama unfold. The earth was proving victorious. The earth was erroneously taking the children first and leaving the adults for last. Soon the children be all gone. It was time for the Kamblas to intervene. To save the children. They were only interested in the children. And of course, the planet. The adults were of no use.

In their weakened state, the humans were unable to resist. They had destroyed any organized government, army or nation. All the countries had broken into millions of fractions and alliances each no bigger than a few hundred. When the Kamblas arrived, the people just watched helplessly.

As the Kamblas entered the earth's atmosphere, their orders were clear. First save the children, from the newborn to the age of sixteen. Anyone older was to be exterminated.

And so it was.

It took a few hours to get rid of eight billion people. Seven years ago they were Forty Billion. Forty billion people was too much for the earth to provide. The human race was fighting for resources and living in deplorable conditions. Mankind had risen from living in caves to living in highly developed cities. They had devised spaceships that toured the solar system. Then he had crumbled back into the caves again. He had gone full circle. They didn't deserve the blue planet. They didn't deserve a brain either. The Kamblas had planned to take over both and had succeeded.

Ruth was there when the invasion happened. The kidnapping of children and the genetic manipulation that followed. As she lay there, she remembered it all. Ruth was taken in a flash of blue light into a spaceship. Many other children were taken too.

Then the genocide followed. The largest genocide of species since the extinction of the dinosaurs. All those people were gone in a matter of hours.

Then it hit her. The first moon isn't a moon at all. It's the mother ship. How did she not realize this before?

She must tell the others, she must warn them. They are all prisoners of the Kamblas. The planet wasn't their home - it was their prison.

She ran as fast as her legs could take her. Why did she come all this way? She was far from the nearest settlement. She took a shortcut through the forest. She knew it well - there was no chance she could get lost. As she ran she wondered if they will believe her. This thought made her stop suddenly. She needed to think about this carefully. She was already some kind of an outcast. Who would believe her? Could she explain exactly how she came to possess such knowledge?

Ruth started walking in the general direction of the village. She wasn't so sure of herself anymore. Her heart was beating fast and the new knowledge was making her feel terrified not liberated. Then she was dizzy again, just like before, she had to lie down to stabilize her head which felt like a stone. And as she drifted off into unconsciousness, she realized her name is not Ruth.

.   .   .   .

Nabi opened her eyes. She was alone in a weird place. It was a small room. The ceiling and the walls were painted in silver. She sat upright. It smelled of nothing. She had never been aware of a lack of smell as she was now. She looked down, she was sitting in a silver bed with silver beddings. The floor was silver too. She looked around. The furniture was silver. The sink was silver and so was the toilet. Only the mirror wasn't silver but everything it reflected was silver. She walked toward the mirror. Her skin colour hadn't changed, thankfully, but she was dressed in a silver-coloured robe. She quickly became aware the silver robe was the only clothing she had. She felt naked. Then terror. Then shame. Who had undressed her? Had she been violated? Where was she exactly? She had a feeling she was being watched. But by whom?

Before she had time to process the situation she was in. Great anxiety began consuming her, she felt dizzy. She had to lie down as her head felt quite heavy. As she drifted off into unconsciousness she wondered how she got here from the pavement and the plant she was trying to uproot. Did she eat that plant? Did she poison herself and now she was hallucinating? Or did she die and she was in heaven? Was heaven silver? Was it……?

When she opened her eyes again, she was still in the same room. She didn't know if she should make any moves at all. She had the same feeling she was being watched. So she just lay there looking up at the silver ceilings. After a while, she felt like using the bathroom, but she fought the urge. After about an hour she couldn't hold it anymore. She went and relieved herself. Then back to the bed again.

She tried to recollect her thoughts. The last thing she remembered was the plant and the pavement. And silver planes and a flashing blue light. And a humming sound. Like distant drums. She tried not to think of her family. She pushed that pain deep into her brain and her heart. And she wasn't sure if she was on earth or in heaven or another dimension. Only now she was sure it wasn't the plant, she never ate it because she never got to uproot it.

There was a soft voice telling her to go to the eating area. Where did the voice come from? She didn't hear it, and yet she heard it. There was no sound. She sat upright, suddenly terrified again. She was shaking. The soft voice came on again. Telling her to get out and go eat something. It was in her head. She was hearing voices. She stopped up her ears with both her hands. But the voice spoke again. She crouched down and buried her head in between her legs. What was happening to her? Was she going crazy?

There was a soft knock on her door. She didn't move. Terror engulfed her again. The door opened slowly. There was another girl standing there. About her age. She spoke softly. It was her voice she had heard in her head. She told her to follow her. And she did.

They went down the hall into a large dining room area. Other kids were already there eating. She felt a sudden sharp hunger pain. She hadn't eaten in ten days. Or was it more? Her hunger pushed aside all fear and soon she was eating the most delicious meal of her life. And there was plenty to eat. Where did all this food come from? There was nothing on earth. This must be heaven.

After filling her stomach, she looked around. Most things were silver-coloured. All the humans in the dining area were children of all races. Dressed in silver-coloured clothes. The same design. As she looked closely, they were mostly teenagers. Where were all the adults? No one was talking. No one was familiar. They were all strangers. After they had their fill, there was the voice again in her head. Telling her to go back to her room. And as she stood up, so did everyone else. They all left and went back to their respective silver rooms. They all heard the same voice in their heads. They all obeyed it.

.   .   .   .

Ruth sat down to eat her dinner. It was her favourite time of the day. When all work is done and she could at last sit and enjoy the sunset. She was unusually drawn to the sunset. What she didn't realize was that all humans on earth were unusually drawn to the sunset. No one ever missed it. Like clockwork, all humans sat and watched as the sun went down and the moon rose up in its place. And today was no different.

She thought about yesterday. She had woken up in the forest. Just after sundown. What was she doing there? Why couldn't she remember? The last thing she knew she was at the edge of a mountain watching the sunset. The next thing she was lying down in the grass in the forest. What happened in between? She seems to have these blank spots in her memory. Almost all of them were of sunsets. She hadn't told anyone. Everyone who talked about memory blackout seems to disappear for a few days, only to come back with their amnesia cured. So she kept her doubts and observations to herself. She didn't have a friend to talk to anyway.

The sun was almost gone now, and the second moon was rising. It had a bluish hue today. How beautiful. The two moons were heading for a collision. An eclipse. how exciting! She sat upright and watched closely. Why was she so excited? The two moons were getting closer and closer and as they touched, she felt faint. Then dizzy, her head was so heavy that she had to support it. She lay back and as the eclipse started, her memory came back.

And she remembered everything. The Kambla invasion, her captivity, the memory wipe out. The genocide, the DNA manipulation. They were slaves in their own planet. She stood upright, she fought the urge to run and tell someone. This happens every evening. If it is happening to her, it must be happening to others as well. She just lay there and let her memory wash over her.

When the eclipse was over, she didn't go into unconsciousness like before. Her memory didn't reset. Something had gone wrong. Then fear and panic set in. She was terrified. The truth remained as clear as the two moons in the sky. She was not Ruth, her name was Nabi. Born and raised in the village of Kadongo. A tiny village in the middle of nowhere in the African continent. Everything came back, both before and after the invasion. The whole timeline of events was as clear as the moon above.

She puked and puked and puked.

· · · · · · · · · ·

Chapter 3

Every evening, all humans on earth were drawn to the sunset, the moon rise and the moon eclipse. They didn't know why. And during the eclipse their memories would come back. Every single one of them remembered their real names, their family members, the invasion, the kidnapping, everything about their past. Everything. And it was terrifying. Some wailed, others ran wildly, many screamed. The air was full of whispers, screams and groans. It was a short moment when the earth as alive with chaos.

Nabi was wrong. She was not alone. Everyone went through this experience every day. The chaos stopped and everyone drifted into unconsciousness only to awaken a few minutes later with no recollection of their past. A memory reset.

Only this evening it was different for Nabi. Her memory didn't reset. She closed her eyes so tightly, desperately wanting to forget her past. Ignorance is indeed bliss. And she longed for bliss. She couldn't handle the truth. Death was better than the truth.

She lay there for hours. The second moon was now out of her sight. The first moon was always there.

And she knew why. Tears started flowing uncontrollably. She coiled herself into the fetus position and sobbed. She was living the most horrible nightmare anyone could have ever invented. A dull pain engulfed her stomach, ejecting her dinner with such force she didn't have time to sit upright. The foul smelling sick went all over her couch and she was powerless to stop it.

Nabi knew if the Kamblas found out the reset didn't work, she will be in great danger. By morning she had resolved to pretend her memory reset was successful.

.   .   .   .

It has been three months now. Nabi has successfully been living a lie. Pretending she didn't remember anything. Pretending her name is Ruth, and like everyone else that she was an orphan. Her vision was normal too. She saw things everyone else wasn't seeing. The small drones that flew by every where. No one seems to notice them, no one talked about them, they were totally invisible to everyone else. Except her. She saw them all the time. The trick was to pretend they were invisible. That was the hardest thing she had to do. Once in a while a drone will stop right in front of her eyes, and she had to continue with whatever she was doing as if it wasn't there.

Then there was the motorbikes. Flying motorbikes. They went up into the mysterious moon and came down again. Female aliens seem to be the only ones riding them. These motorbikes everyone could see them. But they totally ignored them. Sometimes kids would watch them dart across the sky changing direction without losing speed. They had two wheels that never rotated. A strange invention that everyone seems to ignore.

Every evening she acted like everyone else. She acted crazy, sometimes she wept and sometimes she ran out screaming. She kept at it until the eclipse was over. Then she lay down like everyone else and "woke up" when she felt it was safe to do so. She did all she could to fit in and not raise suspicion.

She also kept a secret diary. In the middle of the night when the drones and motorbikes stop their patrols - she woke up and write it all down. She wrote down anything she felt would help her understand the new masters. Anything that could explain why they were here. Especially why did they get their memory back every evening for the length of the eclipse. What was the point in that? Why go into such great lengths to abduct and brainwash them, then restore their memory every day for 20 minutes. This was the Kamblas greatest act of cruelty.

And she knew there must be a reason for it. She would find out. But for now, she must study them, there was a weakness somewhere she could exploit. Patient is the key. They had been patient in taking over the planet, she had to be patient if she would liberate herself.

. . . .

It has been two years now and Nabi was still stuck in living her lie. She had become very good at it. And now she was exhausted by it. She had kept an extensive diary and by now she didn't know which parts of her observations were true and which were her imaginations or just coincidental. She hadn't come close in knowing the reasons behind the evening moon eclipse. she felt ready to do something about it. She didn't know what she will do. But she knew she was ready.

The two years had given her time to come into terms with the truth. The devastating truth about humanity or the little that's left of it. The extinction of all the animals, birds and fish. It was said that cockroaches survive anything, but Nadi hadn't seen a single roach since the invasion. It was a total wipe out of life as they knew it. Only the children survived, solely for the purpose of being turned into slaves. They were divided into two categories, the growers and the miners. The growers were the upper class people. The miners were not. The female growers gave birth to babies, the miners never reproduced. When the children grew up they were designated to be either growers or miners. None had a say in the matter, not even their parents.

Everything the growers cultivated was for their own consumption, and the less quality produce was given to the miners. Everything that the miners worked hard to produce the Kamblas took. That was the main purpose of the human race. There were no other occupations. No artists, scientists, nor inventors. No one was jobless either. Either you worked or you didn't exist. This had been the way of life for 30 years now. Which meant Nabi was nearly fourty-seven years old. And she was Ruth for 30 years, working as a grower. Her speciality was Apples. She was an Apple fruit grower. And it was the only fruit that grew on earth. She remembered all the varieties of fruits that grew before the invasion. Mangoes were her favourite. Juicy mangoes that came in season around the month of January. There were no mangoes now, nor January. They had a different calendar. The months had different names too.

When she was a child she had wanted to be a pilot. The very thought made her laugh. She had her life all planned out when she was 10 years old. She would be a mother of twins - a boy and a girl- and they would live in a house by the beach. They had dreams then, and many dreams did come true. Until they didn't.

Until the day when greedy humans depleted the planet. Until the day when Kamblas came to turn the earth into an investment. Until the day her memory was wiped out and she was a slave. These were the kind of thoughts that dominated her mind these days. And out of them came several ideas - but none was good enough.

Tonight another idea was born. This one was unique. It didn't go away. Like a seed planted on a pot, waiting for the right season to germinate and sprout. The idea sat there on her mind. Churning and turning every day. At first, it was absurd, but every time she thought about it, it was germinating into a brilliant plan. And finally, it sprouted. It was time to jump off the cliff.

The next day she went to work, as usual, selecting a field where the drones were many. She just stood there, didn't work at all. The other growers stared at her, some urged her to do something. But she just stood there, staring straight ahead. She thought of her mother, her brothers and her Aunt. It was time to either join them or go free.

The drone appeared, she thought it was slow, she has been waiting for twenty minutes. It descended down and stopped right at her head. She turned her head to face it. Then smiled at it. And for the first time she talked to it without a word. The way they talked to her in the spaceship 30 years earlier. Telepathically. She finished her message and sat down in the field, stretched her legs out and lay down. She knew what was coming and she was getting ready for it. Her heart was beating fast and she broke into a sweat.

Then the motorbike appeared from thin air. It hovered above her, the rider was this alien woman dressed in silver. She did her best to think about life before the invasion. She visualized eating mangoes, yellow berries and bananas. As expected the motorbike went into a frenzy, circling her body and getting faster with each rotation. More motorbikes appeared. They formed a shield around her. A few minutes later a real spaceship appeared from thin air. All the motorbikes left, there was a flash of blue light and she was beamed up. She felt nothing. Not even the feeling that something was carrying her along. She was simply lifted up and slowly ascended into the mouth of this silver disk. And within what seems like seconds, they were landing on a white-coloured surface. She had been here since the invasion, she remembered it.

She knew what will happen next and was ready for it. That knowledge was her only weapon. As they wheeled her into the building, she remembered the room where they wiped out their memories and implanted new ones. Wiped out her name and gave her a new one. She will not let that happen again this time. She didn't know how she will achieve this, but she knew she mustn't let them win this time round. Her plan was to escape somehow, leave the earth and go to some other planet. Maybe negotiate a deal of release. She had no idea what she will do but she won't allow them to wipe her brain clean.

They put her in a large room, with hollow tubes all around the walls. She knew what the tubes were about. They left her there with only one female. She was busy getting some syringes ready. At the corner of her eye she saw it. It was a red syringe and immediately she knew this was her escape option. She got up so fast catching the female by surprise. Picked up a metal tube on the way and struck her down. Was she really 47 years old? She seem to have a lot of strength. She walked slowly to the far table, picked up the red syringe, and with a slow movement she injected herself with it.

As the liquid spread all over her body she gradually turned invisible. Nabi walked up to the reflective silver walls. She couldn't see her reflection, only floating clothes. She realized she has to go naked. She did.

She walked out of the door locking it as she left. She felt a kind of freedom that was as scary as it was liberating. That dream came back to her, the one about her jumping off the cliff and flying. This is it. She had jumped - but would she fly?

Nabi wondered in and out of many rooms, no one noticed her. She walked into a warehouse with female human bodies arranged in a long row. All pregnant. She walked around trying to figure out if the women were alive. A male alien was working on them, one at a time. She watched for a while. He was injecting their uterus with something. When he ran out of the fluid - she followed him into a large laboratory. This is where they were fast growing the babies. It took three months from conception to labour. Manipulating them so they end up with only two varieties. Growers and miners.

She felt sick and left. Nabi had been here before, she had the injection many times before. And weeks later her body rejected the fetus. For years she thought she was barren. Now she knew something within her was rejecting this unnatural reproduction method. When she was Ruth, she was depressed she couldn't have babies, but now it had turned into a blessing. Something was right within her. Something in her was making it hard to be enslaved in this manner. What was it?

She kept on going from unit to unit. She didn't know how long the serum would work, it was a big risk she was taking. Then she saw something playing on a projector. She went closer. There were a bunch of aliens watching the earth. Zooming in and out of one area to the next. It was an advanced version of Google maps. Very comfortable now with her new superpower, she sat down on the floor at a corner and keenly watched and listened to the discussion. Suddenly she saw something that made her jaw drop.

All around the earth's atmosphere were these rivers. They were invisible to humans, but now she could see them. They flowed from one part of the earth to another, with a network that resembled a fishing net. A fishing net wrapped all around the globe. Miles into the air. And there were boat-like vessels of all sizes sailing on the rivers. Getting on and off wherever they needed. Most of them carried these batteries, these green-coloured batteries, bringing them back to the motionless moon. A few ships carried a mysterious ore that has been mined all over the planet.

She got up and went looking for the boats. She wanted to sail the earth and investigate it further. She went back to the first lab as fast as she could. If she was to leave this moon, she needed more of the red stuff. She found it, found the red serum. As soon as she touched them they turned invisible. She took as much as she could. Putting them in what was once a silver bag, now invisible. This surprised her. Then it dawned on her, if she put on the silver clothing maybe they would turn invisible too. She went looking for some. Found them in the warehouse with the pregnant women. They were all the same size, but of course all the women on earth were of the same size. Another thing that was strange in the new world. She put them on and rushed to the invisible port.

She had found a mission. She jumped into the nearest boat that was about to set sail. As the boat sailed down the river, she felt sick. Was this sea-sick? How long had it been since she turned invisible? She hadn't kept track of time since her first injection. She felt it was running out, and she was right. Within minutes she was totally visible. Quickly she injected herself with more of the red liquid, and waited for it to take effect. Then the worst happened. The alarm went off.

The Kamblas had discovered she was missing. There was a panic back at the moon. The boat was getting further and further away from the moon. And she was getting more and more relaxed. She hoped by the time they figure out what she had taken, she will be long gone.

. . . .

Chapter 4

Nabi was getting an education of her life. For the past one week, she has been all over the planet. She knew what the mining was for. Silver. They seemed to be obsessed with it. They made their spaceships with it. Everything they have had silver in it. She sailed up and down the atmosphere, jumping on and off the boats undetected. She was never hungry nor thirsty, which was a relief.

Today she found out the truth about the moon eclipse. The cruelty of it made her sick. For a long time she thought it was a way of the aliens getting some humour. It wasn't. For twenty minutes each evening humans were nothing more than high charged batteries.

Whenever the eclipse happened a special frequency was released which in turn reset all the memory manipulations they had done on people. As each and every person on earth remembered their past, they went into despair, panic, fear and desperation. And this is what they have been after all along. For a good 20 minutes they harvested these emotions. The whole earth was enveloped by this intense frequency of negative feelings. Kamblas harvested this frequency, converted it into energy and stored it in green batteries. This energy is what they used to power everything they needed. This energy was their main source of existence. Their food, drink and air. They needed it to live. Every Kambla had a green battery inserted at the back of their heads. No bigger than an average thumb. When it ran out - it had to be replaced within minutes or they die. They simply lived on people's fear, anxiety and panic.

On the day of the invasion, they harvested and converted a tonne of batteries, saving their civilization. Now they grew humans to sustain themselves. And every evening they harvested a tremendous amount of it - which they shipped to their planet - Ziwa- at the edge of the galaxy.

The earth was simply a humongous power plant - or a farm - whichever way you preferred to look at it. On the surface it looked like humans had been reduced to either growers or miners. But in reality, they were all food. All of them. Power source that never got sick nor died. Kamblas had fixed the defective gene in humans that used to make them sick, age and die. Now they were immortals in captivity. It was an ingenious plan that had worked perfectly for Kamblas.

Well, perfectly until now.

They had made one fatal error. Either by negligence or by divine intervention, there had been an error that occurred 30 years ago. One of their machines had miscalculated Nabis age. Rendering her Sixteen instead of who she really was - Seventeen. And that was the devilish detail that crumbled an empire that spanned a full galaxy.

The Kamblas knew for their plan to work they could only deal with humans who were no more than sixteen years old. After the human brain was too developed for the mind control serum to work well. They had abducted many humans before and had done extensive research. These experiments lasted for about 100 years before the invasion. It explained why many humans of various ages had mysteriously gone missing over the eighty years before the invasion. The research concluded that the sweet age was sixteen.

When Nabi was abducted her age was miscalculated. This was largely due to the fact she was malnourished. After some years of missing meals, her body had stopped growing. The scanner machine missed to pick up on that and beamed her up instead of killing her. She was the mistake, the error. It explained why she couldn't grow an implanted fetus.

This error became a blessing thirty years later. As she approached menopause, the hormonal changes in her body resisted the frequency manipulations and eventually reset her memory. It started slowly, that is why she had those dreams and visions that got so vivid and intense every passing year. Until one day, everything was reset. And she regained her freedom.

. . . .

The Kamblas were scanning the planet but couldn't detect her. The red serum protected her, but it was running out. It was time. She had jumped. And she had flown. Now it was time to land and face reality. How was she to set herself free? What about humanity? Did they deserve a second chance? After all they had ruined the planet with their greed. The Kamblas were right, anyone who squanders his inheritance didn't deserve another chance.

Something about what the Kamblas had done was sickening. It was one thing to take over the planet earth, but turning humans into batteries was a step too far. This she found hard to forgive.

. . . .

A plan so audacious formed in her mind. And she had only one chance to make it work. The new year festival was the epitome of the Kamblas cruelty. That day the eclipse lasted three hours. It was their biggest harvest day. And everything harvested that day was immediately shipped to the thousands of Kambla bases across the galaxy.

The new year was two days away. It was enough time for her to prepare. She jumped on a boat and went to the largest mine. This was what used to be known as the African continent. It had over one million humans working on it. And because they were many, they had little supervision. The Kamblas may have been patient. But greed was their weakest quality. In their quest for a bigger profit, they overlooked their biggest quarry. That detail had a devil in it too.

The festival went as planned, the miners were enjoying their day off. Ruth wandered around the whole day, going through the plan over and over again. She had never been this lonely in her life. Today she couldn't help envying the humans. They were ignorant and therefore happy. She hadn't been happy since the day her memory reset failed. She doubted she ever will be.

Evening was approaching. The sun was setting, the second moon was rising. By this time she had set herself right in the middle of the festivities. No one knew she was there. She found a pillar, climbed on top of it and got as comfortable as she could. She will be there for three hours.

.   .   .   .

.

Three hours were over. She was surprised it went over time by ten minutes. But she had persevered all through it all. Even during the extra time. She didn't quit until the eclipse was over and the chaos had died down.

All she needed now was patience.

. . . .

The yearly harvest has gone as planned. It was their biggest yet. The quality was the worst. After thirty minutes, humans couldn't produce good quality fear or anxiety. Three hours was a stretch. When they first invaded the earth each new year they harvested for fourty minutes. But the empire was expanding and it was now an enormous beast that had to be fed. It wasn't a time to be fussy. Each new year harvest was sent all over the galaxy. Every planet the Kambla had a base got a large shipment enough to last them another year. Every base was required to put in their orders a few months before the festival. Using this data it was calculated that this year the new year harvest should last three hours and ten minutes.

Ten extra minutes. This was another devil in the detail.

And so it was. The low quality green batteries were sent all over the galaxy. Most of them coming from a huge mine of over a million humans.

With the work now done. Nabi needed patience.

. . . .

Chapter 5

The supervisor on the eastern continent of planet Luwod dropped dead suddenly. The doctors said it was a genetic error. The truth was that it was a malfunctioning battery. Then a child died while playing in the fields of planet Twika. Then another, and then others more. It had started. Isolated cases across their empire. And before long the Kamblas were dropping dead by the thousands. Their space ships were going off course as the pilots died on the job, turning their ships into manic meteorites which in turn killed millions of Kamblas in their home planet. Machinery that depended on the green batteries were malfunctioning causing deaths to millions more. There was panic everywhere.

Quite quickly, very angry Kamblas emerged. Anger has never been a good motivator. Their people demanded an explanation. Their anger fuelled riots and chaos in their home planet. The empire was crumbling very fast. And with all their intellect they couldn't figure out what the problem was. That detail eluded them.

The chaos were happening on planet earth too. On the day Nabi had run out of her red serum - the eclipse had happened as usual. But the two moons didn't separate. They were joined together by some mysterious force. It turned out the supervisor had dropped dead due to a malfunctioning green battery at he back of his head, and therefore accidentally switching off auto pilot button on the eclipse phenomena. All night long the two moons were locked together. Setting humans free for their longest time ever. So long that they quickly formed bands of angry people and started attacking their slave masters. The attack lasted the better part of the night. All machinery were set on fire. The only thing left for the Kamblas to do was to leave.

The Kamblas retreated back into space where they had come from. And the motionless moon went with them.

The earth invasion was swift, and its liberation thirty years later was just as fast.

. . . .

Kamblas were retreating from every planet in the galaxy. One by one each planet was fighting for its freedom. And none lost.

The galactic empire went extinct in one clever move. The Kamblas population swindled to a tiny few. They got on a ship and disappeared from the galaxy.

Ruth watched it happen. It was fast. She hadn't foreseen how fast it will work. She thought she would be captured and killed long before it happened. she had seen the fall of her planet and the fall of an empire all before she was fifty. The rising and setting of suns and moons, of masters and empires. She hoped her people would learn from it.

. . . .

Today they were all free. The planet was a paradise already. They knew how to take care of it. The Kamblas had landed on the earth a hundred years ago. They used the red serum therefore one saw them. After twenty years of study, they started abducting humans. To the police it seemed like random events of missing people. It was far from it. It was calculated kidnapping, for research purposes.

They went a step futher - carefully selected some famous figures for training. They especially concentrated on religious, political and innovation giants. Abducting them without their knowledge and manipulating their desires. Planting one desire specifically on each of them. Greed.

When the most influential of humans are motivated by greed. Evils of immense proportions will soon follow. With that seed planted and carefully cultivated. The invisible Kamblas choreographed the downfall of the human planet. It would take a hundred years. Patience was needed.

Nabis mind was occupied with such thoughts as she sat at her favourite spot. At the edge of her favourite mountain. How could they have missed that detail? Many people claimed they were abducted by aliens. No one believed them. Many more went missing each year. No one cared. Then they elected the worst leaders over and over again. Why? Now she knew why.

Watching the sun set, and the moon rising was still her favourite time of the day. There was no other moon anymore. Just this one. And it was magnificent.

The dreams and visions has stopped. It was over now. She can finally sleep.

And all because of the extra ten minutes of the new year festival.

Firstly, She knew she had to be higher than everyone else. She knew how the harvester machine worked. She had to be on high ground. She had selected the pillar carefully.

Secondly, she had to be right among the humans. That was easy, they all congregated together to watch the sunset on every new year festivals. It has to be camouflaged or it will be detected.

Thirdly, Love was the key. Love is the core of human existence. The motivator for all that is pure and good. The opposite of greed, fear and anxiety. She had to plant her seed of love into the green batteries. A touch of the frequency of love would kill a Kambla flat on contact.

Now this last detail surprised her. Without the extra time, the seed wouldn't have germinated and produced fruitage. Three hours was not enough. Who would have known the extra ten minutes was the last devilish detail that brought down an empire.

With the Kambla gone, their influence over humans was gone too. The human race will innately love each other and love their home. They are the best custodians of the blue planet.

.   .   .   .

As she sat there enjoying the moon rise. Nabi thought she had it all figured out.

She was unaware of the main reason why she succeeded.

There was no devil in this one. She was a woman. There isn't a powerful emotion on earth as a woman's love. The intensity of it took dominance over the feelings of fear and anxiety. A female's love - by design - was unique in its frequency, it was superior to a male.

That was the divine detail. And a divine secret.